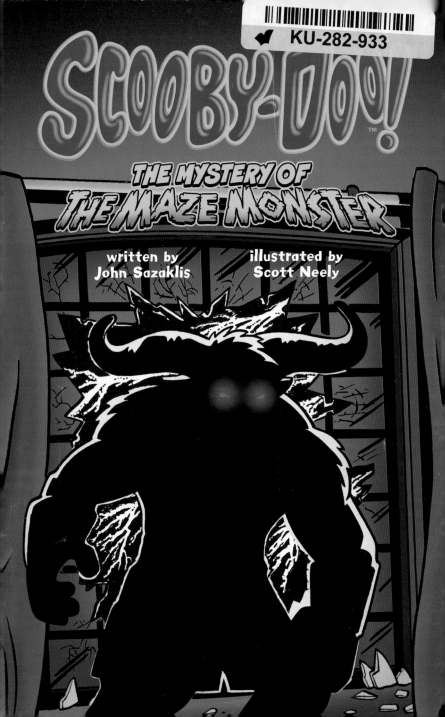

SCOOBY-DOO!

THE MYSTERY OF THE MAZE MONSTER

written by
John Sazaklis

illustrated by
Scott Neely

THE MYSTERY INC. GANG!

SCOOBY-DOO

SKILLS: Loyal; super snout
BIO: This happy-go-lucky hound avoids scary situations at all costs, but he'll do anything for a Scooby Snack!

SHAGGY ROGERS

SKILLS: Lucky; healthy appetite
BIO: This laid-back dude would rather look for grub than search for clues, but he usually finds both!

FRED JONES, JR

SKILLS: Athletic; charming
BIO: The leader and oldest member of the gang. He's a good sport – and good at them, too!

DAPHNE BLAKE

SKILLS: Brains; beauty
BIO: As a sixteen-year-old fashion queen, Daphne solves her mysteries in style.

VELMA DINKLEY

SKILLS: Clever; highly intelligent
BIO: Although she's the youngest member of Mystery Inc., Velma's an old pro at catching crooks.

SCOOBY-DOO!

A monster is hiding in a business tycoon's maze garden! Only YOU can help Scooby-Doo and the Mystery Inc. gang solve this maze mystery.

Follow the directions at the bottom of each page. The choices YOU make will change the outcome of the story. After you finish one path, go back and read the others for more Scooby-Doo adventures!

YOU CHOOSE the path to solve...

THE MYSTERY OF THE MAZE MONSTER

On a dark and stormy night, Minos King, the eccentric shipping tycoon, sits in his candlelit study. He wears an expensive silk kimono and reads *Successful Businessman Magazine*.

Lightning flashes and thunder rumbles.

Mr King heads towards the window. He pulls the velvet curtains back to peer outside. The rain patters rapidly against the pane.

The elderly gentleman squints and focuses on a tall, leafy wall.

I hope my new garden can withstand this terrible weather, thinks Mr King.

Then he sees a shape shift in the darkness.

Turn the page.

That's impossible!

The tycoon hurries into the hallway and calls for his help. Wadsworth, the British butler, comes running from the dining room. Yvette, the French maid, dashes out of the kitchen.

"What is it, Master Minos?" Wadsworth asks.

Mr King catches his breath. "There's someone in the garden! Sound the alarms, call the–" Mr King stops and stares at Wadsworth.

The butler's tailored tuxedo is glistening with drops of water. His shoes are wet, leaving a puddle on the Persian rug.

"Why are you wet, Wadsworth?" Mr King asks.

"I asked him to take out the rubbish," Yvette offers. "I was not going out in that weather."

"Yes, sir. I'd just come in from the east wing when I heard your cries," Wadsworth replies.

"I saw someone in the garden," Mr King bellows. "Why haven't the motion detectors gone off?"

"I'll go to the security control room and check it out," Yvette says. "The storm must have interfered with the sensors." She runs down the hall, her high heels clacking against the tiles.

"Sir, I shall check the fuse box in the maintenance room. Perhaps there is a faulty circuit," Wadsworth says and rushes towards the cellar door.

Mr King is left alone in the foyer.

"Hmm . . . I wonder where I should go?" he says out loud.

SKEEEEESH!

The tycoon is startled by the sound of breaking glass.

"To the gallery!" shouts the master of the house.

Minos King is quite sprightly for an old man. Within seconds, he reaches the dark chamber where he keeps many valuable and ancient artefacts.

Mr King fumbles for the light switch.

Turn the page.

"Where is that blasted thing?" he curses.

Another sound echoes through the darkness.

GRRRRROOOOAARR!

Mr King's blood runs cold.

He turns to see two glowing red eyes staring at him. Lightning crashes, outlining the silhouette of a hulking brute. Mr King glimpses two polished white horns on top of a bull's head. Steam puffs out of its nostrils. The rest of its body is that of a muscular man with hooves instead of feet.

GRRROOOARR!

The creature swipes at the billionaire with a massive paw, knocking him down. Then it hurtles over the billionaire, crashing through another window. *SKEEEEESH!*

Moments later, Mr King feels a strong set of arms lift him up. The lights flicker on, and he is facing Wadsworth and Yvette.

"What happened?!" they ask.

Turn to page 12.

"I was attacked by a . . . a . . ." Mr King searches for the right word. "Minotaur!"

The servants exchange looks.

"The mythical creature from ancient Greece, sir?" Wadsworth says.

"Don't look at me like I have ten heads," Mr King says with a huff.

"No, sir, that would be the Hydra."

The billionaire grabs the butler by the lapel and points to the far wall. The large display case that housed many priceless relics is now empty.

"I've been robbed blind, and that creature is the culprit!" he shouts.

"What do we do?" Yvette asks, clearly shaken.

"Isn't it obvious, my dear?" replies Mr King. "We get Nedley Blake on the phone!"

"At this hour, sir?" Wadsworth asks.

"YES!"

The butler pulls out his mobile phone and dials Mr King's best friend.

He hands the phone to his employer.

"Blake?" barks the billionaire. "Minos King here. Is your daughter, Daphne, still working with those kids? The ones that meddle? Good. Send them over first thing in the morning. Now go back to bed, Blake. It's late!"

Mr King hands the phone to Wadsworth.

"Never you fear, my friends," he says, looking confident. "The daring detectives of Mystery Inc. are on the case!"

***

The next day, the Mystery Machine cruises up the long, winding driveway leading to Minos Manor. Driving the green van is Fred. In the front seat sit Daphne and Velma. Rounding off the gang is Shaggy and his hound, Scooby-Doo.

The vehicle stops at a leafy wall of vines. Extending to the left and right is a tall hedge.

"Like, Daphne, are you sure this is the right place?" Shaggy asks. "Because it looks like we've hit a dead end."

Turn the page.

"Reah, red end," Scooby-Doo agrees.

"Of course," Daphne replies. "My family has known Mr King for years, and we visit often. This is his new garden maze."

"Garden maze?" Fred asks. "Is that what this thing is?"

"Yup," Velma adds. The clever detective downloads a recent article onto her tablet computer. "It says here that Minos King, retired billionaire, built a hedge maze on the property around his massive mansion to ensure the protection of the King fortune. The living labyrinth's many paths, twists, and turns were designed in such a way that any intruders or unwanted guests would get lost for days."

"Days!" Shaggy gasps. "I hope we packed enough snacks, Scoob!"

"Re, too!" Scooby says.

Suddenly Mr King appears from a hidden entrance in the maze. "Thank you for coming," he calls out to Daphne.

He approaches the Mystery Machine and looks inside. "Lovely to meet your friends," he says. "Would you like to go straight to work or have a quick bite? My staff has prepared a large lunch for you!"

If the gang heads to the scene of the crime, turn to page 16.

If the gang stops for lunch first, turn to page 32.

"Thank you for the kind offer, Mr King," Fred says, "but lunch can wait."

"Rit ran?" asks Scooby, grabbing onto his grumbling stomach.

"Yeah, like, I'm starving," adds Shaggy.

"Well then, the faster we solve this case, the sooner we eat," Daphne suggests.

"Sounds like a plan," says Velma.

"Then follow me," the tycoon replies. "I'll lead you through the labyrinth."

"Jinkies," Velma says, marvelling at the maze. "This is quite a structure."

"Yes, I hired an architect named Ms Daedalus to build it. She's the best in the business and a dear friend."

"I'm a big fan of her work," Velma replies.

After what seems like an endless journey, the mansion finally comes into view.

"It's as beautiful as I remember," Daphne says as the group enters.

"Wow, really groovy," Fred adds.

"Right this way," Mr King says. He guides the gang into the gallery and points to the shattered display case. "This is where I encountered the – ahem – Minotaur."

"Zoinks!" cries Shaggy. "Like, did he just say Minotaur?!"

"Yes, my boy," Mr King says. "Some mazes have cheese in them, but I guess mine has a Minotaur."

"Oh, we like cheese!" Shaggy replies, and Scooby-Doo wags his tail.

Fred, Daphne, and Velma approach the display case. On the shelves are placards and labels that identify all the artefacts.

"Velma, log these in so we have an inventory of what's missing," Daphne says.

"Good idea," Fred adds and starts reading off the roster: an Incan idol, a Grecian urn, a bronze scimitar, a crouching tiger statue, and a crystal skull. He goes on and on.

Turn the page.

Velma types away on her tablet computer. Finally she says, "Jinkies, this is an archaeological scavenger hunt!"

Meanwhile, Shaggy follows Scooby-Doo. The Great Dane sniffs his way to the broken window.

"Like, you followed your nose to our first clue, buddy," Shaggy exclaims.

Scooby-Doo points with his paw. "Rook at this!" he says.

Shaggy picks up a clump of fur caught in the windowpane. It is dark brown and very coarse.

"I'm really hoping this is yours," Shaggy says to Scooby-Doo.

"Ruh-uh!" the dog says, shaking his head no.

Shaggy swallows hard. "Like, maybe this monster is real after all."

Scooby-Doo looks up at the large hole in the window and adds, "Rand real BIG, too!"

"Hey, you guys," Shaggy calls out. "Come and see this!" He holds up the fur.

"Jinkies," Velma says. "A clue!"

"Whatever was in here last night probably left a trail," Daphne says.

"I bet you we'll find it if we search outside," Fred states.

"Good idea," Velma replies. "Let's go!"

The members of Mystery Inc. walk back outside the mansion and stand under the broken window. There are big muddy footprints in the wet grass. They lead right into the garden maze.

"Double jinkies!" Velma exclaims. "More clues!"

"Let's follow these tracks," Fred says.

The gang heads into the maze, and soon they reach a fork in the road. To the left is a straight path. To the right, the path curves behind a hedge wall.

SNAP!

Scooby-Doo's ears perk up at the sound of a cracking branch.

Turn the page.

"Ruh-roh!" Scooby says and points to the hedge wall.

The leaves begin to shake. The gang hears rustling footsteps coming their way. They huddle closer together.

"Zoinks!" Shaggy cries, trembling. "It's the Minotaur! What do we do?"

If the gang runs left, down the straight path, turn to page 35.

If the gang runs right, towards the footsteps, turn to page 21.

"I'll tell you what we'll do," Fred says. "We'll get to the bottom of this case. Charge!"

The gang runs towards the rustling footsteps. They turn the corner and see a tall figure coming their way. His face is covered, and he is carrying a stack of boxes.

"Jeepers, those must be the stolen relics," Daphne says.

"Get him!" Fred commands. Together they pounce on the mystery figure.

"OOF!" grunts the stranger, tumbling to the ground. The boxes topple and pour out their contents. Maps, blueprints, catalogues, and books scatter everywhere.

When the group untangles themselves, they discover the stranger is just another teenager like them.

"Hey, why'd you do that?" he asks, brushing dirt off his jeans.

"Oops, sorry," Daphne says. Then she leans over to Velma and whispers, "Gosh, he's cute!"

Turn the page.

"Like, you're not a monster," Shaggy says.

"Well, depends who you ask. My mum thinks I'm a terror," the teen chuckles. He extends his hand. "Name's Icarus, but you can call me Russ."

"Nice to meet you, Russ," Fred says, shaking his hand. Then he introduces himself and the members of Mystery Inc.

The friends help Russ pick up his belongings.

"What brings you to Minos Manor?" Velma asks.

"Well, Mr King hired my mum to design this garden maze a while back. She's an architect, and I'm her assistant," Russ answers. "This morning he called us over to bring the map and blueprints."

"Like, it's a good thing we found you when we did," Shaggy says. "There's a Minotaur in this maze, and we need to find the nearest exit!"

"Did you actually see a creature that's half man and half bull?" Russ asks suspiciously.

The gang exchanges looks.

Fred says, "Uh, no."

Russ lets out a loud laugh. "Ha! You've been reading too many Greek myths before bed."

He picks up his boxes and says, "If you'll excuse me, I have work to do."

The Mystery Inc. gang watches Russ walk away.

If they follow Russ out of the maze, turn to page **28**.

If they continue their investigation, turn to page **35**.

"Jeepers," replies Daphne. "The mysteries keep piling up around here."

"The loud sound came from the driveway," Mr King says to the gang. "Follow me."

Once the billionaire and the Mystery Inc. gang reach the driveway, they find another car parked next to the Mystery Machine. The bonnet is popped open and puffs of grey smoke billow out from the engine. A teenage boy fans the air with his arms.

"Icarus, is that you?" Mr King asks.

The boy turns around and smiles. A white toothy grin appears within a grease-smeared face. "Hi, Mr King!" he says. "Mum and I are just having a bit of car trouble."

A stylish woman exits the car. "Sorry to frighten you," she says. "The car backfired. Luckily my boy here knows a thing or two about mechanics."

"Everyone, this is Ms Daedalus and her son, Icarus," Mr King says.

Icarus wipes a greasy hand on his jeans and extends it to Daphne. "You can call me Russ," he says with a grin.

Daphne keeps her distance. The thought of all that grease and oil on her designer dress is unbearable. "Charmed," she says.

Fred shakes Russ's hand and introduces the gang. "We're here to help Mr King solve a mystery!"

"We're here to help, too," Russ says. "My mum designed the garden maze. She's an architect, and I'm her assistant."

"Jinkies," Velma says. "I'm a fan of your work!"

"Thank you, my dear," replies the architect. "It is one of a kind."

"Yes, quite right," Mr King interrupts. "So were my prized possessions. And they were stolen by a menacing monster!"

Suddenly the ground begins to rumble and there is a low grumbling sound.

Turn the page.

"Ronster!" Scooby-Doo cries.

He jumps into Shaggy's arms.

A large shape lumbers up the drive. It is an all-terrain sports utility vehicle.

"That's not a monster," Fred says. "That's a monster truck. Groovy!"

Out of the driver's seat jumps a burly, barrel-chested man. He is wearing a pith helmet, combat boots, and safari gear.

Slinging a tranquilizer rifle off of his shoulder and into his hands, he cocks it and announces, "I'm hunting me some Minotaur!"

"Excellent," Mr King says. "The gang's all here. Ladies and gentlemen, meet Dr. Martin Clark, archaeologist and professor. He originally discovered the artefacts that were in my private collection."

"How do you do?" Martin says, tipping his hat.

"I gathered you here to help get my treasures back," Mr King says. "Are we ready to go?"

"Like, we work better on a full stomach," Shaggy says. "Does anyone have anything to eat?"

If the group goes into the maze to hunt the Minotaur, turn to page 63.

If the group goes into the mansion for a formal lunch, turn to page 57.

The members of Mystery Inc. follow Russ out of the maze and back to the driveway.

They find another car parked next to the Mystery Machine. The bonnet is popped open and puffs of grey smoke billow out from the engine. A stylish woman in a business suit with a pencil in her bun is standing next to Mr King.

"Hi, Mr King," Russ says. "Mum sent me into the maze to find you. We were having a bit of car trouble."

"Well, I came running as soon as I heard that explosion," Mr King replies. "It was loud enough to wake my ancestors."

"Sorry to frighten you," the woman says. "The car backfired and gave us all a jolt."

Mr King turns to the group and says, "Everyone, this is Ms Daedalus. You've already met her son, Icarus."

Velma says, "I'm a fan of your work!"

"Thank you, my dear," replies the Ms Daedalus. "It is one of a kind."

"Yes, quite right," Mr King interrupts. "So were my prized possessions. And they were stolen by that menacing monster!"

"Monster?" Russ says, raising an eyebrow. "These kids mentioned a Minotaur, but I thought they were just mad. Are you serious?"

"Yes!" Mr King answers. "That big brute is the bane of my existence. It's why I called you all here. There's still one person missing, though."

As if on cue, an all-terrain sports utility vehicle comes rumbling up the drive.

Out of the driver's seat jumps a burly, barrel-chested man. He is wearing a pith helmet, combat boots, and safari gear.

Slinging a tranquilizer rifle off of his shoulder and into his hands, he cocks it and announces, "I'm hunting me some Minotaur!"

"Excellent," Mr King says. "The gang's all here. Ladies and gentlemen, meet Dr. Martin Clark, archaeologist and professor. He discovered the artefacts from my private collection."

Turn the page.

"How do you do?" Martin says, tipping his hat.

"Now let's go back to the mansion to discuss my plan," says the billionaire. "We will also enjoy a nice meal in the dining room."

Scooby's ears perk up. "Rining room? RET'S GO!"

Turn to page 54.

"LUNCH? That's the magic word!" Shaggy cries. He and Scooby-Doo leap out of the van. They run towards Mr King and shake his hand.

"Rub-a-dub-dub, where's the grub?" Shaggy asks. He and Scooby-Doo are both drooling.

Mr King chuckles and guides the members of Mystery Inc. through a hidden entrance in the garden maze. After numerous twists and turns, they reach a fancy picnic shelter.

In the centre is a long table with a giant feast. Standing next to it is Wadsworth, the butler.

"We've prepared a small meal for your guests, Master Minos. There's roast turkey, mashed potatoes, mixed greens salad, corn on the cob, and candied yams."

"Small meal?" Fred exclaims. "It looks like Thanksgiving dinner at all our houses combined."

"Like, we'll certainly be giving thanks for all this food, won't we, Scoob?" Shaggy says.

"Rhat's right!" Scooby says. "Rhank you!"

Turn to page 34.

Quick as a flash, the two friends dive face-first onto the table and inhale everything in sight.

Scooby-Doo stretches his mouth open wide and devours the turkey whole. A split second later, he spits out the bones.

"Rummy in my tummy," he says, patting his belly.

Suddenly a loud explosion startles the group.

KA-BOOM!

"Good heavens," shouts Mr King. "What on Earth could that be?"

If the gang follows Mr King towards the sound, turn to page 24.

If the gang runs into the mansion, turn to page 40.

The gang continues their investigation by taking the straight path down to another clearing. Inside the open space stands a grand structure made of sparkling white marble.

"Like, I sure hope that's a really fancy snack stand. I'm starving!" Shaggy says.

"Re, too!" Scooby says, rubbing his stomach. "Ry tummy's rumbling!"

"That's not a snack stand. It's a mausoleum," Velma explains. "It's a large tomb for Mr King's deceased relatives."

"Jeepers," Daphne says. "I sure hope we don't meet any of them. We don't need ghosts as well as a Minotaur."

"Speaking of which," says Fred, "aside from a fur patch and some muddy footprints, what evidence do we have that he really exists?"

Velma shoots him a look. "Fred, how long have we been in this business?"

Before Fred can answer, the group hears a low grumble.

Turn the page.

"Like, I sure hope that was your tummy, Scoobs," Shaggy says.

Scooby-Doo shakes his head no.

The sound gets louder and turns into a growl. "GRRRRR!"

Then they hear a *THUMP, THUMP, THUMP,* like thundering footsteps.

The friends jump and huddle together in the corner of the clearing.

"It's coming from the other side of this hedge," Velma whispers. "If only we could see over it!"

Shaggy turns to Scooby and says, "Okay, buddy, time to put Plan Periscope into effect!"

"Rye-rye, Raptain!" Scooby-Doo says and salutes his friend.

Shaggy squats down low while Scooby climbs onto his back. The Great Dane stretches his neck like a periscope and peeks over the hedge. He scans the perimeter from left to right.

Turn to page 38.

All Scooby-Doo can see is the top of the maze. It consists of hedges, leaves, vines, a pair of horns, and some branches.

"Rorns?" Scooby-Doo wonders aloud.

The horns shift upward, and Scooby-Doo is snout to snout with the Minotaur.

ROAAAAAAR!

"Rinotaur!" Scooby-Doo cries. "Re's real!"

Suddenly sharp claws slice through the hedge. They tear through the thick vines like tissue paper, shredding them to bits.

The Minotaur stands face to face with Scooby-Doo. The hound's jaw drops in fright.

A massive furry paw lunges for Scooby-Doo. His hind legs pinwheel so fast they bop Shaggy on the head a few times.

SMACK! THWAP! WHACK!

The cowering canine hides behind Fred and Daphne. The Minotaur roars again as he rips the leafy wall apart.

"ZOINKS!" Shaggy shouts. "Like, this guy sure knows how to make an entrance!"

Daphne gasps. "What do we do now?"

If the friends run for it, turn to page 44.

If the friends hide in the mausoleum, turn to page 48.

"We don't need to go looking for trouble," Shaggy says.

"Rhat's right!" Scooby-Doo agrees.

"We'll wait for you inside," Daphne says to Mr King.

Wadsworth leads the team towards the mansion.

"Like, we should stock up, Scoob," Shaggy says. "Just in case."

"Rof course!"

The two friends head back to the table. Scooby-Doo lifts up one end, and the food slides down the other. Shaggy is waiting with open arms to scoop up the delicious pile.

He makes sure to balance everything carefully so it doesn't fall. The candied yams rest on top of the corn on the cob, which rests on top of the mixed greens salad.

"This should hold us over until we get to the mansion," Shaggy says.

"Ri rope so!" Scooby-Doo says, licking his lips.

Then he and Shaggy run to catch up with their friends.

Turn the page.

Wadsworth leads the way to the mansion. It is a tall, beautiful building that is hundreds of years old. They enter the grand foyer.

"I love this place," Daphne says. "There are so many rooms!"

"Indeed, Ms Blake," Wadsworth says. "You're welcome to trade places with me and clean them if you like."

Daphne pats him playfully on the arm. "Oh, Wadsworth, you're so funny!"

The dry British butler doesn't crack a smile, but instead ushers the group towards the kitchen.

"Bonjour," says the French maid. "I am Yvette. So nice to meet you."

"It's nice to meet you, too," the gang says.

Yvette holds up a tray. "I have prepared some *hors d'oeuvres* for you."

Shaggy leans over to Velma and whispers, "Is that something we can eat?"

Velma chuckles.

Then she explains, "Yes, Shaggy. *Hors d'oeuvre* is the French word for 'starter'."

"Like, they sure look appetizing," Shaggy says and takes the tray from Yvette.

He and Scooby-Doo tilt back their heads and pour the contents into their open mouths. Their cheeks puff out to the limit.

At that moment, Mr King walks in with three other guests.

Wadsworth clears his throat and says, "Those *hors d'oeuvres* were for everybody!"

Shaggy and Scooby-Doo's eyes widen as they gulp the food down their gullets.

"Oops," Shaggy says.

"Rorry," Scooby-Doo adds.

"Oh, nonsense," Mr King exclaims. "There's plenty more where that came from. Let us go to the dining room, and I'll introduce my guests."

Turn to page 53.

As the Minotaur slashes through the hedge, the five friends turn tail and escape down the nearest path. They run as fast as their legs can carry them. The Minotaur gives chase.

THUMP! THUMP! THUMP!

Scooby-Doo looks back and sees the monster gaining on them. Big, hairy hooves pound the ground as steam billows from his nostrils.

"Ruh-roh!" Scooby cries. He jumps onto Shaggy's back.

The friends follow the twisting path until they reach . . . a dead end!

"ZOINKS!" Shaggy exclaims.

"We're trapped!" Daphne shouts.

"Let's think of a plan – and quickly," Velma says. "The Minotaur is getting closer."

"I've got it!" Fred announces. "We'll make a human ladder and climb over the hedge."

The Minotaur is just around the corner.

Shaggy hops onto Fred's shoulders.

Turn to page 46.

Fred threads his fingers together, making a step for Velma. She puts her foot on his hands and hops up onto Shaggy's shoulders. Daphne follows. Then they wait for Scooby-Doo to climb up next.

"Scooby-Doo, where are you?" the friends ask.

They teeter and totter, slowly losing their balance.

"ROARRR!"

The Minotaur has cornered the canine. He grabs at Scooby-Doo, who slips under the monster's hooves and runs towards the gang.

The Great Dane climbs up the human ladder and reaches the top of the wall. He loops his tail around Daphne's arms and yanks, hoisting his friends into the air and over the hedge.

They land in a heap and tumble all the way down a high hill. When they finally reach the end, everyone gets up and dusts themselves off.

"Phew, we made it! Great job, everybody," Fred says.

"Not that great," Daphne replies. "Look up."

The members of Mystery Inc. stare at the mansion at the top of the hill.

"It looks like it's a mile away," Shaggy complains. "Now we have to start all over again."

"I'm not walking all the way back," Daphne says, sitting on a log. She pulls her mobile phone out and starts dialling. "Let's see if Mr King can send a limo for us."

The rest of the gang takes a seat and waits.

"All is not lost," Velma says, reaching into her bag. "I found some Scooby Snacks!"

Scooby-Doo licks his lips and says, "Scooby-Dooby-Doo!"

THE END

To follow another path, turn to page 15.

"I've got an idea," Fred whispers. "Follow me, gang."

He points towards the mausoleum and signals for the others to keep quiet by putting a finger to his lips. Fred, Daphne, Velma, Shaggy, and Scooby-Doo tiptoe to the tomb.

The Minotaur continues to tear his way through the hedge wall.

When the friends reach the mausoleum, Fred pulls on the heavy door handle.

"Drat!" he says. "It's locked."

"Jeepers," Daphne says. "How are we going to get inside?"

"Like, leave it to Scoobs!" Shaggy says.

"Rhat's right," Scooby-Doo agrees. He pops out a claw and sticks it into the keyhole. He jiggers his finger up and down and side to side, sticking out his tongue for concentration. Then suddenly, **CLICK!** The lock pops open.

"Ra-da!" says Scooby, taking a bow.

"Great job, Scooby!" Velma says.

She reaches into her bag and hands the dog a Scooby Snack. He gobbles it up and licks his lips. "Rummy!" he says.

Finally Fred pulls the tomb door open, and the gang clambers in. They push it shut, lock it, and lean against it with all their weight.

ROOAAAAR!!

Outside they hear the Minotaur roaring angrily. He's torn through the wall, and his thundering footsteps rattle the mausoleum. Spiderwebs and dust shake loose and rain down on the gang.

A spider lands on Shaggy's head. It crawls down onto his nose, and he opens his mouth to scream.

Thinking quickly, Scooby-Doo puts his paw over Shaggy's mouth, stifling the cry.

The spider hops off of Shaggy's nose and lands on Scooby-Doo's paw. Scooby's eyes go wide and bulge out of his head.

Turn the page.

He opens his mouth to scream, but Velma clamps it shut with her hand.

"Shhh!" she whispers and brushes the spider away. "Stay calm, and I'll give you a Scooby Snack."

"Rokay," Scooby-Doo says.

If the gang stays in the mausoleum, turn to page **78**.
If they go back outside, turn to page **51**.

Once it is quiet, Fred unlocks the door and peeks outside. "The coast is clear," he says. Then he steps out. Seconds later he bumps into a mysterious figure.

CRASH! OOF!

"Ouch!" Fred cries.

"Good heavens!" exclaims the figure. "What are you doing here?"

"Wadsworth!" Daphne says. "What are *you* doing here?"

"Mr King sent me into the maze to find you, Ms Blake. That's not as outrageous as hiding in a crypt!" replies the butler.

"Jeepers," Daphne exclaims. "We were hiding from the Minotaur!"

"He's real?" Wadsworth asks. He looks shaken but quickly regains his composure. "Why don't we go back to the mansion and get to the bottom of this?"

"Sounds like a wonderful idea," Velma says.

Turn the page.

"Rexcuse me," Scooby-Doo says, tugging on her sleeve. "Ry Scooby Snack, please."

Velma throws the treat up in the air and Scooby-Doo gobbles it up.

Turn to page 42.

Once everyone has entered the lavish dining room and taken their seats, Mr King continues the introductions. His first guests are a stylish woman in a business suit with a pencil in her bun and a teenage boy in a hoodie and jeans.

"Ladies and gentlemen, may I present Ms Daedalus and her son, Icarus."

The young man turns to the group and says, "You can call me Russ."

"I am the architect who designed the garden maze," Ms Daedalus says. "Russ is my assistant and junior designer."

"Nice to meet you," the gang says.

Mr King then introduces a burly, barrel-chested man wearing a pith helmet and safari gear.

"This is Dr Martin Clark, the archaeologist who discovered the ancient relics. He's also a professor."

"That's me," says the big man. "Martin's my name, and excavating's my game."

Turn the page.

"Mr Clark has found precious artefacts from all over the globe. Most end up in museums, but some get snatched up by brilliant billionaires like myself!" Mr King says with a laugh.

"That must be really exciting, sir," Fred says to Martin.

"It sure is," replies the professor. "One of the missing items is an Incan idol made of Peruvian turquoise. It was found at the ancient city of Machu Picchu many years ago after an ancient temple was discovered."

"That sounds fascinating," Velma says. "Tell us more."

"I'd love to!" Martin declares.

BEEP! BEEP! BEEP!

"Pardon me," says the archaeologist. He retrieves a small digital device from his pocket. "I have to take this call."

Martin excuses himself from the room.

Yvette and Wadsworth also leave the room in order to bring in the meal.

Turn to page 56.

Meanwhile, the teenagers make small talk with the other guests. All of a sudden, the room plunges into darkness.

"Like, who turned out the lights?" Shaggy moans.

"That's odd," Mr King says. "What's the meaning of this?"

Ms Daedalus and Daphne take out their mobile phones. They use each screen's light to illuminate the area around them. Daphne rummages through her bag and finds a torch.

"This should help us!" she says.

If the gang searches for a way to fix the lights, turn to page 60.

If they wait for the electricity to return on its own, turn to page 66.

Everyone enters Minos Manor and heads to the lavish dining room.

Inside, Wadsworth and Yvette are waiting to greet the guests. The Mystery Inc. gang stops to take in the lavish room. A long table surrounded by tall chairs sits in the centre. On one wall is a ceiling-high bookcase, and on the other is a fireplace lined with gold candlesticks. Many priceless paintings adorn the walls.

Once the guests have taken their seats, Fred turns to Martin. "I bet what you do is really exciting, sir," Fred says.

"It sure is," replies the professor. "Did you know that one of the missing items is an Incan idol made of Peruvian turquoise? It was found in a temple at the ancient city of Machu Picchu many years ago."

"That sounds fascinating," Velma says.

"What's more fascinating," Mr King continues, "is that I've invited my dear friend Ned's daughter, Daphne, and her colleagues to do what they do best. Solve mysteries!"

Turn the page.

There was a round of applause for the Mystery Inc. gang.

"Now tell us more about this monster, Minos, old chap," Martin says to Mr King. "Does he really have glowing eyes and horns?" The professor lets out a loud belly laugh. "I've hunted many beasts in my day, but never a mythical one. And inside a labyrinth, no less! I shall change my name to Theseus, slayer of the Minotaur, when this is said and done. HA!"

Fred turns to Martin and asks, "Can you tell us more about your beast hunting days?"

BEEP! BEEP! BEEP!

"Pardon me," says the archaeologist. He retrieves a small digital device from his pocket. "I have to take this call."

Martin excuses himself from the room. Yvette and Wadsworth also leave the room in order to bring in the meal.

Meanwhile, the teenagers make small talk with the other guests.

Then, all of a sudden, the room plunges into darkness.

"Like, who turned out the lights?" Shaggy moans.

"That's odd," Mr King says. "What's the meaning of this?"

Ms Daedalus and Daphne take out their mobile phones. They use each screen's light to illuminate the area around them. Daphne rummages through her bag and finds a torch.

"This should help us!" she says.

If the gang searches for a way to fix the lights, turn to page 60.

If they wait for the electricity to return on its own, turn to page 66.

Daphne turns on her torch and shines the beam around the room. She spies five gold candlesticks on the mantle of the fireplace.

"Aha! We'll light those candles until we fix the power," she says.

"Brilliant idea, dear," Mr King says. "I should have some matches right here in my pocket."

While Mr King searches his coat, the Mystery Inc. gang head over to the fireplace. They each grab a candlestick.

Shaggy grabs the last candlestick, but it won't budge.

"Hmm, I think it's stuck. Help me out, Scoob," he says.

"Rou got it!" Scooby-Doo says. He puts his arms around Shaggy and pulls.

Mr King finds the matches and looks over at the fireplace. "Wait, not that one!" he cries.

It's too late. Shaggy and Scooby-Doo yank the candlestick so hard that it breaks off with a piece of the mantle attached.

The candlestick is really a lever. Gears shift from inside, turning the entire structure around on a revolving platform.

In the blink of an eye, Shaggy, Scooby-Doo, and their friends disappear from the dining room. They find themselves inside a secret chamber.

"Jeepers!" Daphne says.

She points the torch into the room. Dusty old furniture are piled up on top of each other, and there are several stacks of boxes.

"Is anyone hurt?" calls Mr King through the dining room wall.

"We're fine," Fred yells back. "Where are we?"

"You're in an old storage room," Mr King replies. "That last candlestick is a lever that provides access. Just pull it down again, and you'll come right back."

"Oh, it's been pulled down, all right," Shaggy says holding it up. "And broken off right in my hand."

Turn the page.

"I see," Mr King says. "Well then, sit tight. We'll get you out somehow!"

The members of Mystery Inc. take a seat on top of the old boxes and wait to be rescued.

"I'm sorry, you guys," Shaggy says. "At least we're all in here together. Safe and sound."

Just then, behind a pile of boxes, a pair of glowing red eyes appears.

THE END

To follow another path, turn to page 15.

The group decides to head into the maze to hunt the monster. Before they leave, Fred reaches into his pockets and turns them inside out, searching for food. Some loose change and lint falls out.

"Sorry, guys," he says. "I've got a whole lot of nothing."

Daphne rummages around in her bag. "How about some strawberry flavoured lip gloss?" she asks Shaggy and Scooby.

"Hmm, that might taste good," Shaggy says.

Suddenly Scooby-Doo nudges his friend. "Randwiches, remember?"

Shaggy slaps his forehead. "Gosh, Scoob. You're right. Like, I made sandwiches!" The scatterbrained teenager reaches into his own pockets and pulls out two sandwiches.

"We've got ham, cheese, pickles, and mayo, buddy. Enjoy!"

The hungry friends scoff them down in less than five seconds.

Turn the page.

"Enough bellyaching," Martin says. "Let's hunt ourselves a Minotaur!"

"Brilliant," Mr King says. He and Ms Daedalus lead the way.

Russ, Fred, Velma, Daphne, Shaggy, and Scooby-Doo follow along.

Martin takes the rear with the trusty tranquilizer rifle at his side.

"I sure feel safer with him around," Shaggy says to Scooby-Doo.

"Re, too," replies the Great Dane.

Walking trough the maze, the group encounters many twists and turns. Some paths are easier to navigate than others. Finally they reach a clearing with a fork in the path.

"If we go left, we'll reach the mausoleum," Ms Daedalus says. "If we go right, we'll find the fountain."

"I say we go to the mausoleum," Martin states. "Sounds like the perfect place for a monster to hide."

"Like, take it from us, it's a great hiding spot," Shaggy replies.

"Okay, so which way do we go?" Daphne asks.

If they go to the mausoleum, turn to page 71.

If they go to the fountain, turn to page 76.

"Nobody panic," Mr King says. "I remember this happened last night with the storm. Wadsworth is probably on his way right now to check the fuse box in the cellar."

"We'll just wait in the dark and be patient," Ms Daedalus says.

"There's no need for that," replies a voice.

Yvette enters from the kitchen holding two lit candles. She walks over to the fireplace and lights the candlesticks on the mantle. Then she lights the candelabra on the dining room table.

The room fills with a warm glow.

"Thank you, Yvette," Mr King says. "You are always full of bright ideas!"

Suddenly the dining room door swings open, revealing a tall, dark figure.

"Is that Wadsworth or Martin?" Mr King asks.

Then he sees red eyes staring back at him.

"The Minotaur!" he gasps.

The monster roars and charges into the room.

It grabs an empty chair and hurls it at the wall. *SMASH!* The chair splinters into tiny pieces.

Everyone screams.

"Looks like we have a pretty angry party crasher!" Shaggy gulps. "Like, let's get out of here!"

Yvette, Ms Daedalus, and Russ run into the kitchen and lock the door.

The Minotaur charges again, this time right towards Mr King and the members of Mystery Inc.

"Quickly, my friends, this way!" shouts the tycoon.

If they follow Mr King to the fireplace, turn to page 68.

If they follow Mr King to the bookcase, turn to page 83.

Mr King leads them to the fireplace and pulls the last candlestick on the mantle. It is really a lever that reveals a hidden entrance.

The fireplace is on a revolving platform that turns as the Minotaur approaches. Before the monster can reach them, the group is transported into a secret chamber.

The Minotaur pounds on the wall, but the friends are safe.

"Phew!" Fred says, wiping his brow.

"That was some quick thinking," Velma adds.

"Where are we?" Daphne asks. "I've never seen this room before!"

"It's a secret passageway that takes us alongside all the rooms on the east wing to the back of the manor."

The group follows the passageway until they reach the end. They are at a landing with two staircases. One leads up. The other leads down.

"Jinkies!" Velma says, pointing to a dirt pile. She pulls out her magnifying glass and kneels.

Daphne shines her torch over the new clue.

Velma discovers that the dirt is mixed with shards of glass.

"This glass matches the broken window in the gallery. And the dirt is dry mud from the garden. Whoever committed the crime came back here last night."

Daphne tracks the dirt with the beam from the torch. "And they went all the way up these stairs. Where do they go?" she asks.

"The attic," Mr King replies. "But I haven't been up there in years."

"Which makes it a great hiding place for a crook," Fred adds.

CLANG. CLANG.

A metallic banging sound echoes up the lower staircase.

"Like, did you hear that?" Shaggy asks.

Suddenly the noise gets louder.

CLANG! CLANG!

Turn the page.

"Rhat is it?" Scooby-Doo asks. He starts to tremble and hugs Shaggy.

"It's coming from the cellar," Mr King says. "Someone is banging on the pipes to get our attention!"

"What do we do?" Daphne asks.

"That's easy," Fred replies. "We split up and investigate!"

To follow Velma, Shaggy, & Scooby-Doo to the cellar, turn to page 90.

To follow Fred & Daphne to the attic, turn to page 87.

"Let's follow Martin," Fred says.

"Outstanding!" bellows the burly man. He leads the way.

"If I didn't know better, I'd say you were star-struck, Fred," Daphne whispers to him.

Fred chuckles. "He may not be a film or rock star, but he's still a celebrity to me."

The group takes the left path and heads towards the mausoleum. The gleaming marble tomb comes into view.

"What a beautiful building," Ms Daedalus says.

"It's for a beautiful woman," Mr King replies. "Dearly departed Mrs King, my wife."

"Jinkies, look!" Velma says, pointing to the door. "The padlock has been broken."

"Why exactly are we here, Clark?" Mr King asks the professor.

"Simple, Minos," Martin says. "Your crook probably got lost in the maze."

Turn the page.

Martin continues, "He needed to hide the stolen goods until he could come back and get them. This is the perfect hiding spot."

Mr King enters the crypt and inspects it. He finds a leather satchel tucked away behind a marble column. The tycoon looks inside, discovering the stolen items.

"By Jove, he's right! My valuables *are* here!" Mr King declares.

Everyone cheers and thanks Martin Clark for his ingenious suggestion.

"How did you know that, Martin?" Fred says.

"That's easy," the archaeologist answers. "I'm a professor. I know everything!"

"The case is solved. We can all go back to our lives!" Mr King says. "Thank you all. I'll make sure to reward each and every one of you."

"Sir, what about the Minotaur?" Velma asks.

"Bah! I probably imagined the whole thing. That's what you get for eating too many midnight snacks," Mr King replies.

"You can never eat too many midnight snacks," Shaggy says.

"Rhat's right!" Scooby-Doo agrees.

As the group heads back to the driveway, Velma pulls Daphne aside.

"Something doesn't add up," she whispers. "Follow me."

As the billionaire bids his friends farewell, the girls of Mystery Inc. sneak onto the bed of Martin's truck. They find a toolbox under a tarp.

"Double jinkies," Velma says. "Look!"

"There's a clump of fur caught in the latch," says Daphne. "The same fur we found in the gallery."

Velma opens the toolbox and finds wire cutters, a crowbar, and a map of the maze.

CLUMP! CLUMP! CLUMP!

Suddenly they hear Martin's boots clomping towards the truck. The girls hop out of the back as the driver starts the ignition.

Turn the page.

"This Dr Clark isn't the only beast hunter around here," Velma says. "We're going to give him a taste of his own medicine."

The girls head back to the Mystery Machine and tell their friends about Martin's mischievous plot.

"What a load of bull!" Fred exclaims and slams on the gas. "He's not getting away this time!"

"ZOINKS!" Shaggy cries. "Like, here we go!"

The Mystery Machine burns rubber and disappears in a cloud of dust.

THE END

To follow another path, turn to page 15.

The group follows the path to their right and heads to the fountain. It is a beautiful bronze sculpture of a mermaid holding a conch shell to her lips, blowing it like a horn. A stream of water spurts from the shell and trickles to the base below.

"I had this fountain commissioned by an artist in Denmark," Mr King says. "Isn't it lovely?"

"It sure is," the group agrees.

Suddenly the sky starts to darken as thunderclouds creep up around the sun. In a few minutes, it is completely overcast.

"Ruh-roh," Scooby-Doo says.

"Scooby's right, guys," Shaggy says. "I think we need to shake a leg – or paw – and find some cover."

BOOM!

Thunder crashes, and lightning flashes across the sky. The clouds unleash a torrential downpour on Mr King and his guests.

"This way," Ms Daedalus shouts over the storm. The group follows the architect in search of protection from the elements. "There's a gazebo nearby!"

Standing under the wooden structure, the members of Mystery Inc. stare out at the garden maze while the rain pours down.

"Well, this certainly puts a damper on our investigation," Fred says.

THE END

To follow another path, turn to page 15.

For now, the gang decides to stay in the mausoleum.

"It might be safer here in the tomb," Fred says.

"Like, I'd rather take my chances with the spiders than the Minotaur," Shaggy says.

"Re, too!" barks Scooby-Doo.

Daphne shines her torch around. The light reflects off of spiderwebs, casting abstract shadows on the surrounding walls. In the centre is a crypt, and some marble columns stand around it.

"Wow," she says. "It's really pretty, in a creepy sort of way."

WHOOOOOOOOOOOOOO!

A howling sound whistles through the mausoleum, and the friends huddle together. Scooby-Doo grabs on tightly.

"Rhat ras rat?" asks the frightened hound, shaking like a wet dog.

Shaggy's teeth chatter, and his knees knock together with fright. "Like, did we wake up the ghost?" he asks. "Turn off your torch, Daph. It's trying to sleep!"

"It's not a ghost, Shaggy," Velma says. "It's just the wind blowing through the cracks." She shines her torch on the dusty walls of the mausoleum. The cobwebs hanging in the corners are fluttering from a light draft.

"Rokay," Scooby-Doo says. The curious hound walks over to Daphne and trips over something. "Roops!"

Scooby-Doo bumps into Daphne, who bumps into Fred, who falls onto the crypt. The slab slides over a few inches.

"AHHH!" the kids yelp.

"Jinkies!" Velma cries. "There's something looped around Scooby's paw."

"What is it?" Fred asks.

"It's a leather strap, and it leads right into the crypt," Velma says.

Turn the page.

Together the friends slide the slab a little more to see where the strap leads. It is part of a satchel.

Lifting it out of the crypt, Fred dusts it off and calls out to Daphne. "Shine your torch here, please," he says.

The beam of light reveals the satchel's contents: the Incan idol, Grecian urn, bronze scimitar, crouching tiger statue, and crystal skull. All the items stolen from Mr King's collection of priceless artefacts!

"We found the goods!" Fred exclaims. "This must have been the Minotaur's hiding spot. Too bad we didn't catch him, though."

"Well, if he's still out there, I'm staying in here," Shaggy says.

"I have an idea, gang," Velma exclaims. "I'll use my laptop to send a signal to the Minos Manor security system. I'll let Mr King know we're here with the goods, and he can come and pick us up."

Turn to page 82.

"Good idea," Daphne says.

"In the meantime, let's have some Scooby Snacks to celebrate," says Shaggy.

Scooby-Doo agrees. "Scooby-Dooby-Doo!"

THE END

To follow another path, turn to page 15.

Mr King leads the gang towards a bookcase on the far wall of the dining room.

"Watch this," the crafty tycoon says.

He pulls on a thick leather-bound book. Gears shift and whir within the wall. The bookcase slides sideways on a track to reveal a hidden exit leading out to the garden maze.

"Run for safety," Mr King demands. "I'll handle this overgrown fur ball!"

The youngsters dash forward into the maze. As the Minotaur charges towards the group, the billionaire sticks out his cane under the monster's feet. Tumbling horns over hooves, the Minotaur lands headfirst in the mud.

The gang cheers at Mr King's heroic move, but the victory is short-lived.

"ROOAR!" The Minotaur is back on his feet and bounding for the members of Mystery Inc.

The gang heads into the maze, and Fred pulls them behind a tall hedge. He looks up at a low-hanging tree branch, and his face lights up.

Turn the page.

"I've got an idea," he says. "We're going to make a trap to catch the Minotaur." Then he looks at Shaggy and Scooby-Doo and says, "And you're going to be the bait."

"Ro way!" barks Scooby-Doo.

"Like, what he said?" Shaggy adds.

"Would you do it for some Scooby Snacks?" Velma asks.

The Great Dane hesitates and says, "Rokay."

"Here's the plan," Fred says. He picks up a long, thick vine and ties a lasso at the end of it. "We're going to loop this over that tree branch so it lands on the other side of the hedge. Daphne and Velma will cover up the lassoed end with leaves and then join me back here."

"Jinkies!" Velma exclaims. "I get it! So when the Minotaur runs onto the disguised lasso, we'll pull the vine tight, trap his hoof, and hoist him up into the air."

"Exactly!" Fred says, smiling proudly. "Isn't it groovy?"

ROAR!

The gang hears the Minotaur approaching and springs into action.

"You're on, boys," Daphne says to Shaggy and Scooby-Doo.

"Take these Scooby Snacks and run," Velma tells the duo. "Don't forget to leave a crumb trail to find your way back to us!"

"Like, it's now or never, Scoobs," Shaggy says.

"Ret's go!"

The hapless heroes run out from hiding, right into the path of the Minotaur! The menacing monster gives chase. Shaggy and Scooby-Doo run like mad, all the while munching on Scooby Snacks.

From behind the hedge, Fred, Daphne, and Velma can only imagine what is happening. They hear whimpering, growling, and rustling through the foliage.

Suddenly the vine pulls taut in Fred's hands. The trap has been activated.

Turn the page.

"We got something!" Daphne cries.

The three friends pull with all their might, yanking their prey high into the air. Fred loops the vine around the tree trunk and ties it with a triple knot.

"Great job, gang," he says. "That criminal is high and dry!"

If the friends go see whom they've captured, turn to page 99.

If they wait for Shaggy & Scooby to return and go together, turn to page 97.

Fred and Daphne follow the muddy footprints up into the attic.

They duck their heads below the low-hanging ceiling. All around they see old furniture and boxes.

A trail of dirt and broken glass leads to a partially hidden trunk.

Fred finds an oil lamp and some matches. He lights it, casting a warm glow over the room and illuminating the trunk. The flickering flames cause shadows to creep and dance on the walls like ghosts.

"Look, Fred," Daphne says. "More clues!" She points to the clump of fur caught on the hinge of the trunk.

Fred crouches near the trunk. He says, "Open the trunk. I bet you whatever is inside will be a break in this case!"

Daphne unhooks the latch and slowly opens the trunk. The lid lifts back to reveal . . . the Minotaur's head!

Turn the page.

Daphne lets out an ear-piercing scream. "AHHHHHH!"

Fred almost drops the lantern from fright. He brings the light closer to the head.

"Jeepers, Daphne," Fred says. "It's a rubber mask. The Minotaur is a fake!"

Fred hands the lamp to Daphne and pulls out the mask. There are mechanics inside that make the eyes glow and the nostrils blow steam. Folded beneath it is the rest of the Minotaur costume.

"Well, looks like we solved one mystery," Daphne says. "But we still don't know who's the real menace behind the mask."

"And where the stolen valuables are hidden," Fred adds.

"Let's go and find the others and get to the bottom of this," says Daphne.

Fred agrees and blows out the lantern. The two friends bundle up the costume and take it with them.

Then they head downstairs to the cellar. The work of Mystery Inc. is never finished!

THE END

To follow another path, turn to page 15.

Velma, Shaggy, and Scooby-Doo take the stairs down to the cellar.

CLANG!

CLANG!

CLANG!

The clanging sound gets louder as they approach. Velma finds a light switch and flicks it. A single uncovered bulb shines light on the dingy, musty cellar.

In the far corner of the room, near the boiler, someone is sitting on a chair. As the friends walk closer, they discover that it's a person who has been gagged and tied.

Velma adjusts her glasses and squints into the dim light ahead. "Jinkies!" she exclaims. "It's Martin Clark!"

The intrepid archaeologist has managed to free his feet and kick against the iron pipes with his heavy boots. The sound has been travelling all the way up the side of the house, alerting the members of Mystery Inc.

Velma quickly pulls the gag off of Martin's mouth. "Could you give me a hand, Scoob?" she asks her four-legged friend.

"Row 'bout ra rooth?" replies Scooby, grinning widely with his shiny, white teeth.

CHOMP! CHOMP!

He chomps down onto the ropes and chews through them with ease.

Once the ropes fall to the ground, Shaggy helps the professor to his feet.

"Like, what happened, big guy?" Shaggy asks.

"My head's still a little hazy," answers Martin, "but I remember leaving the dining room to answer my phone. Then I was ambushed from behind and woke up here!"

"Rouch!" Scooby-Doo replies.

"I thought I was still dreaming," Martin continued, "but I could have sworn I saw a creature that was half man and half bull shutting down the power from that fuse box over there."

Turn the page.

"That must have been the Minotaur," Velma explains. "He's been the cause of all the trouble here at Minos Manor."

"Like, let's get out of here before he shows up again," Shaggy says nervously.

Suddenly a ferocious growl echoes off the cellar walls.

"ROOARRRR!"

"ZOINKS!" Shaggy cries in alarm. "We're too late!"

Red eyes glow in the darkness, and the Minotaur charges into the light. The beast lunges for Scooby-Doo with all his might.

"Not on my watch," cries Martin. "Heads up!"

He picks up a wrench and hurls it at the Minotaur. The monster ducks, and the wrench scrapes a pipe, ripping the metal.

Hot steam blasts out of the pipe, right into the Minotaur's face. Disoriented, the monster lumbers forward and trips over Scooby-Doo.

Turn to page 94.

WHAM!

The creature lands headfirst into the wall, where his horns get stuck in the bricks.

"Like, that's using your head, Scoob!" Shaggy says.

"He's trapped!" Velma cries.

Together the friends pull the Minotaur off the wall, but his head stays stuck. It's really a mask!

"This monster is a fake," Shaggy says.

"And it's none other than Wadsworth!" Velma announces.

"Great Caesar's ghost," Martin exclaims. "The butler did it!"

Before Wadsworth can escape, the archaeologist uses the same ropes to tie him up. "Sit tight," he says to the crook.

At that moment, Fred and Daphne arrive with Mr King and the other guests.

"Wadsworth?!" Mr King gasps. "I'm shocked. What is the meaning of this?"

"Bah!" shouts the butler with disgust. "I was going to sell those precious artefacts on the black market and use the money to retire on a warm, tropical island."

"You mean, these precious artefacts?" Fred asks.

He holds up a leather satchel containing the stolen items.

"They were hidden in a trunk in the attic," Daphne says. "Your muddy footprints led us right to them!"

"And, like, the only place you'll be retiring is to prison," Shaggy adds.

The gang smiles.

Wadsworth snarls and says, "It was a perfect plan. And I would have gotten away with it, too, if it wasn't for you meddling kids!"

Mr King sighs and says, "Good help is so hard to find these days. Luckily the members of Mystery Inc. are great at what they do. I'm glad I decided to call on you."

Turn the page.

"Especially Scooby-Doo," Shaggy says. "He's the one who stopped the menace of the Minotaur."

Scooby-Doo smiles and says, "Scooby-Dooby-Doo!"

THE END

To follow another path, turn to page 15.

Fred, Daphne, and Velma remain hidden behind the tree. Their plan worked. They caught the Minotaur!

Huffing and puffing, Shaggy and Scooby-Doo come scrambling around the hedge.

"Like, did we catch him or what?" Shaggy asks.

"Let's go and see," Fred says.

The five friends sneak around the tall maze wall and come to the entrance of the path. Right in the middle is a figure hanging upside down from the branch.

Creeping closer, the members of Mystery Inc. discover that the person in the trap is . . .

"Mr King!" cries Fred.

"Jeepers!" Daphne exclaims. "How could you be the Minotaur?"

"I'm not the Minotaur, child!" the tycoon shouts. "Cut me down from here before all the money falls out of my pockets!"

Turn the page.

After the friends release Mr King from their trap, he tells them how he followed the sound of the commotion into the clearing.

"I saw that terrible monster chase you down this path, and so I came along to help," Mr King stated. "Then, before I knew it, the world turned upside down!"

"Sorry about that," Fred says.

"Like, if you're not the Minotaur, that means he's still out there," Shaggy says nervously.

"Ruh-roh," Scooby-Doo adds. "Rhere he is!"

The friends turn to see the Minotaur standing behind them. His eyes glow red and steam puffs out his nose. He is blocking the only way out of the maze.

"Zoinks!" Shaggy cries. "Like, we're doomed!"

THE END

To follow another path, turn to page 15.

Fred, Daphne, and Velma sneak slowly around the hedge. They see a mysterious shape dangling in the air, lassoed by the vine. Numerous appendages flail at its side while the creature howls.

"AROOO!"

Upon closer inspection, the friends discover what the creature really is . . .

"Jeepers!" gasps Daphne. "We caught Scooby and Shaggy!"

The two friends are tangled together and hanging upside down from the branch. Sweets, treats, and snacks tumble out of Shaggy's pockets.

"Like, your trap certainly works, Fred," Shaggy says, twirling around above him. "I feel like a *piñata*!"

"Drat. I thought we'd got the Minotaur," Fred said, letting out a sigh. "I guess he got away!"

Suddenly a dark shadow falls over the gang.

"Ruess again!" Scooby-Doo shouts. Still

Turn the page.

hanging in the tree, he hugs Shaggy tightly and closes his eyes.

The others turn around to see . . .

The Minotaur!

His red eyes glow. Steam puffs out of his nostrils like two exhaust pipes. The beast scrapes his hooves against the ground, readying himself to charge at any moment.

"ROAARR!" The monster lets out a terrible roar that echoes through the night.

"Jinkies!" Velma cries. "I've got an idea. Run for it!"

Fred, Daphne, and Velma race down the path back to the tree. The Minotaur gives chase, stampeding after them with powerful, lightning-quick speed.

"This time, Fred and I are going to be the bait," Velma says to Daphne. Then she leans over and whispers the rest of the plan into her friend's ear.

THUMP

THUMP

THUMP

The Minotaur clears the hedge and pounds down the path. Daphne hides behind the tree, disappearing from view.

"Hey, fur ball!" Fred shouts. "Catch us if you can!"

He and Velma sprint down the path. The Minotaur roars, spins on its heels, and takes off after them.

In the meantime, Daphne pulls out a nail file from her purse. She begins to slice away at the vine tied around the tree. It slowly unravels.

Fred and Velma run back around to where they left Shaggy and Scooby-Doo. The Minotaur is hot on their heels.

Approaching their friends, they both shout, "NOW!" They dive for cover.

Daphne cuts through the vine.

In a flash, Shaggy and Scooby-Doo fall from

Turn to page 103.

the branch. They come crashing down right on top of the monster!

WHAM!

The monster is pinned to the ground beneath Shaggy and Scooby. The beast kicks and bucks, but he cannot move beneath the weight of the two friends. Luckily they both had a hefty breakfast this morning.

"Zoinks!" Shaggy cries. "Looks like we got the Minotaur after all."

"GRRRRR!" he snarls.

At that moment, Mr King arrives with the other guests. They had followed the sound of the commotion.

"The Minotaur!" Ms Daedalus says in alarm. "He's real!"

"He's a real fake!" Fred says, ripping off the Minotaur's mask.

Mr King gasps when he sees the monster's true identity. "Martin Clark! But why?"

Turn the page.

The professor struggles to free himself, but the combined weight of Shaggy and Scooby-Doo is too heavy to move.

"Those artefacts are worth a fortune!" Martin spits out. "If I had sold them, I would be living in a mansion bigger than this one."

"Well, the only big house you'll be staying in is prison," Shaggy says.

"Reah!" Scooby-Doo agrees.

Wadsworth walks over and announces, "I've alerted the authorities, and they are on their way."

"Excellent news," Mr King says. "A great big thanks goes out to the members of Mystery Inc. for solving another case."

"Do you have anything else to say, Dr. Clark?" Fred asks.

"My Minotaur plan was flawless," he snarls. "I would have got away with it, too, if it weren't for you meddling kids!"

"Famous last words," Daphne says.

"And so are these," adds Velma, pointing to Scooby-Doo.

Grinning from ear to ear, the Great Dane replies, "Scooby-Dooby-Doo!"

THE END

To follow another path, turn to page 15.

AUTHOR

John Sazaklis, a *New York Times* bestselling author,
enjoys writing children's books about his favourite
characters. To him, it's a dream come true. He has
been reading comics and watching cartoons since
before even the Internet was invented! John lives
with his beautiful wife in New York, USA.

ILLUSTRATOR

Scott Neely has been a professional illustrator
and designer for many years. For the last eight
years, he's been an official Scooby-Doo and Cartoon
Network artist, working on such licenced properties
as Dexter's Laboratory, Johnny Bravo, Courage the
Cowardly Dog, Powerpuff Girls, and more. He has
also worked on Pokémon, Mickey Mouse Clubhouse,
My Friends Tigger & Pooh, Handy Manny, Strawberry
Shortcake, Bratz, and many other popular
characters. He lives in a suburb of Philadelphia and
has a scrappy Yorkshire Terrier, Alfie.

GLOSSARY

abstract (ab-**STRAKT**) – based on ideas rather than things you can touch or see

eccentric (ek-**SEN**-trik) – unusual or strange, but in a harmless or amusing way

ensure (en-**SHOOR**) – to make sure that something happens

foyer (foy-**AY**) – an entrance hall or walkway

hapless (**HAP**-lis) – unlucky or unfortunate

idol (**EYE**-duhl) – an image or object that is worshipped

ingenious (in-**JEEN**-yuhs) – inventive and original

intrepid (in-**TREP**-id) – very brave, especially when exploring something unknown

inventory (**IN**-vuhn-tree) – a complete list of items

mausoleum (maw-suh-**LEE**-uhm) – a building that contains a tomb or tombs

periscope (**PER**-i-skope) – a vertical tube containing prisms or mirrors and lenses that allows you to see an object far above you or behind an obstacle

scimitar (**SI**-mih-tur) – a sword with a curved blade

tycoon (tye-**KOON**) – a very wealthy and powerful businessperson

What do you get if you cross a Minotaur with a yeti?

a. An abomina-bull snowman!

b. A frost biter!

c. Chilli beef!

How do you get out of a maze?

a. Pick up a bat, get three strikes, and you're out!

b. Hitch a ride on the mino-tour bus!

c. Act bored, and then you'll never be a-mazed.

What do you call a sleeping Minotaur?

a. A bull-dozer!

b. A Mino-snore!

c. Nothing – it's herd it all before!

What did Shaggy say when he ran into the Minotaur?

a. "If I don't leave now, my life's at steak."
b. "Bye, son!" (bison)
c. "Love to stick around, but I'm not a-bull!"

What musical instrument does a Minotaur play?

a. French horn
b. Cym-bulls
c. Cowbells!

What is the favourite snack of Greek monsters?

a. Gorgon-zola
b. Cheese and krakens
c. Neptuna fish sandwich

LOOK FOR MORE...

← YOU CHOOSE STORIES →

SCOOBY-DOO!

THE CHOICE IS YOURS!

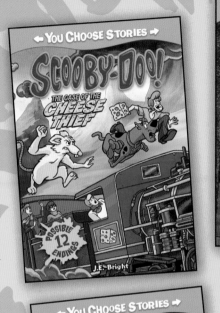

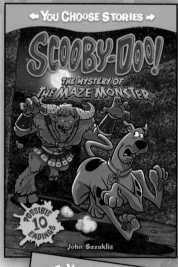